Hooray for Thomas!

•AND OTHER THOMAS THE TANK ENGINE STORIES•

Random House 🏠 **New York**

A Random House PICTUREBACK® Book

Photographs by David Mitton, Terry Palone, and Terry Permane for Britt Allcroft's
production of *Thomas the Tank Engine and Friends*

Thomas the Tank Engine & Friends®

A BRITT ALLCROFT COMPANY PRODUCTION
Based on The Railway Series by The Reverend W Awdry
© 2005 Gullane (Thomas) Limited

A HIT Entertainment Company
All rights reserved under International and Pan-American Copyright Conventions.
Published in the United States by Random House Children's Books, a division of Random House, Inc., New York,
and simultaneously in Canada by Random House of Canada Limited, Toronto.

www.randomhouse.com/kids/thomas   www.thomasthetankengine.com

Library of Congress Control Number: 2004095617

ISBN 0-375-82876-1 Printed in the United States of America First Edition 10 9 8

• Hooray for Thomas! •

It was an exciting day on the Island of Sodor.

"Good morning," called Harold.

Annie and Clarabel were full of happy children. Thomas was taking them to their annual Sports Day. Everything was ready for the day to begin.

"I do hope I'm Number One and win a medal," said a boy.

"It must be splendid to win a medal," chuffed Thomas. "After all, I'm Engine Number One!"

Thomas worked hard all afternoon. But he couldn't stop thinking about medals. He imagined himself wearing a gold medal on a bright red ribbon. How smart he would look!

"Hello, Thomas," whistled Percy. "I'm taking Sir Topham Hatt to Sports Day."

"You can see the egg-and-spoon race," chuffed Thomas.

"I didn't know eggs and spoons had races."

"The *children* race with eggs on spoons," said Bertie.

"And the winner gets a medal— I wish *I* could have a medal."

"You need to win a race first!" whistled Percy.

"*I'll* race you, Thomas. The first one to the station is the winner!"

"You're on," called Thomas.

"Ready,
        steady,
            GO!"

"Better hurry, Bertie!" peeped Thomas.

Then Thomas had to stop to pick up some passengers.

"Better hurry, Thomas!" teased Bertie as he rattled over the bridge.

Then Bertie had to stop at a level crossing.

"Last one there puffs hot air!" called Thomas.

Thomas was nearly at the station.

As he drew near the playing field, a signalman flagged him down. Now Thomas was really cross. Bertie was sure to win.

Then he saw Sir Topham Hatt.

"Thomas, the Sports Day medals have been left in my office. You must fetch them at once. We can't let the children down."

"Of course not, Sir," replied Thomas. And he chuffed away.

Meanwhile, Bertie had raced into the station.

"I won!" shouted Bertie. "I won!" And he waited eagerly for Thomas. He waited and waited.

But Thomas had forgotten about the race. He was thinking about the children.

"I can't let them down . . . I can't let them down."

At last, Thomas puffed back into the big station. The Station Master gave Thomas' Driver the box of medals.

Then Thomas set off again.

He arrived *just* in time!

"Well done," said Sir Topham Hatt.

"Thank you, Sir," panted Thomas.

Sir Topham Hatt presented the medals to the winners.

"Congratulations!"

"Thank you, Sir!"

The next day, Bertie and the medal winner arrived with a surprise for Thomas.

A small boy presented *him* with a gold medal on a red ribbon.

"You were very helpful at Sports Day."

"So we thought you should have a medal of your own," added the boy.

"My very own medal!" said Thomas. "Thank you."

"Three cheers for Thomas, the Number One Engine! Hip, hip, hooray!"

"But I still won the race," tooted Bertie.

· The Grand Opening ·

The engines on the mountain railway were excited.
They were helping to build a new line.
 It would take visitors to even more beautiful
places on the Island of Sodor.

Sir Topham Hatt arrived with important news. "The Grand Opening is this afternoon. I want to see the new line from the air. Lady Hatt and I will arrive on Harold the Helicopter."

Just then, Skarloey chugged in.

"You're late for the announcement," complained Sir Topham Hatt. "Really Useful Engines are never late."

"I'm sorry, Sir."

At the airfield, there was another problem.

"Engine trouble," said the Pilot. "Harold's not going anywhere today."

Lady Hatt was most upset. "But I've been looking forward to the Grand Opening all week."

"And I, my dear, will find a solution."

And he did.

"Topham, you cannot be serious. Me, ride in this?"

"The wind direction is perfect. We'll be there in no time."

Soon the hot-air balloon rose into the sky.

But Skarloey was upset. "All this extra work is going to make me late again!"

The hot-air balloon was floating peacefully through the sky.

Lady Hatt was enjoying herself. "The new line looks splendid!" she said.

"Thank you, my dear," replied Sir Topham Hatt.

Down the track, the workmen were still loading their ladders.
"Hurry up, hurry up," Skarloey puffed.

"If Skarloey doesn't
hurry," sighed Sir Topham
Hatt, "he'll be late again!"

All the engines were ready for the Grand Opening.

"Where's Skarloey?" Rusty asked.

"He promised to be on time," said Peter Sam.

At last, Skarloey was on his way.

Then there was trouble. The balloon's flames suddenly went out. The air in the balloon cooled and the balloon started to fall.

"Hold tight," the Pilot called.

"I want to get out," demanded Lady Hatt.

"Not now, dear," said Sir Topham Hatt.

"The balloon's going to land in the tree," cried Skarloey.

And it came down right in front of Skarloey.

"There's Sir Topham Hatt."

"My hat is ruined," cried Lady Hatt.

"So is mine," said Sir Topham Hatt.

"Don't worry!" called Skarloey's Driver. "We'll soon have you down."

"Am I glad to see *you*, Skarloey."

"Thank you, Sir."

Before long, Sir Topham Hatt and Lady Hatt were safely on the ground. They boarded Skarloey's boxcar and set off at once.

Everyone was waiting as Skarloey brought his important passengers to the Grand Opening.

Sir Topham Hatt declared the new line open.

"With special thanks to Skarloey," he said, "for helping us get here!"

Everyone cheered.

"Even so, you were *still* late!" teased Rusty.

"I know," said Skarloey. "But because I was late, Sir Topham Hatt was right on time!"

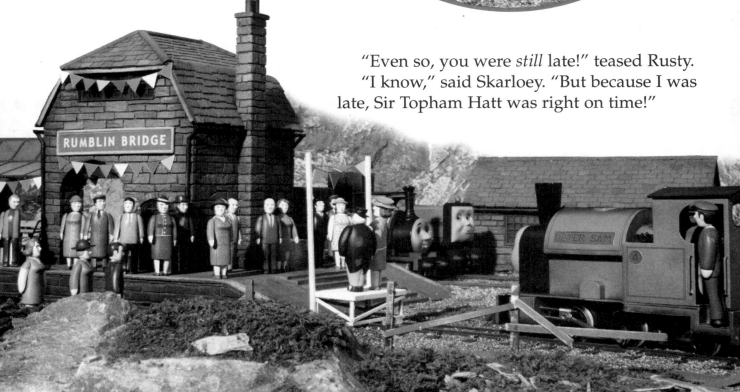

• Best Dressed Engine •

It was May Day on the Island of Sodor and the engines were celebrating. They knew there'd be music and lots of fun.

The station was being decorated. Sir Topham Hatt said that the engines could be decorated, too.

"I'm going to have flags and streamers!" whistled Percy.

"I'm going to have a big red banner," whistled Thomas.

"What decorations will you have, Gordon?" asked Murdoch.

"Decorations aren't dignified for an important engine like me. I pull the Express!" Gordon was feeling insulted. "Humpf! Silly little engines," he grunted.

Thomas was enjoying himself. He was bringing the maypole.
The farmer's children waved. Thomas peeped happily as he
passed by.

Soon it was time for the
decorating.
Percy's Driver was
wrapping streamers and
flags around his funnel.
Thomas had a big red
banner on his tanks.

Even Murdoch was being decorated. Although he was very shy about it.

"We could have a contest for the Best Dressed Engine," suggested James.

Just then, Gordon shunted in. "A contest!" he puffed. "I'm bound to win any contest."

"You will have to be decorated," said James. "This is a Best Dressed Engine contest."

"Not me!" puffed Gordon. "You'd never catch *me* looking so ridiculous!"

The engines felt splendid.

But not Gordon . . . he was cross. "Decorations aren't dignified. Hah! Who cares about a contest anyway?"

Further down his line, a colorful banner was strung across the bridge.

Then, as Gordon steamed across the bridge, it came loose and wrapped around his firebox. Gordon couldn't see the line ahead!

Gordon tried to whoosh the banner off, but it wouldn't budge.

"I can't see!" he whistled loudly to his Driver. "Stop!"

"You *can't* stop, Gordon," his Driver called back. "You're the Express!"

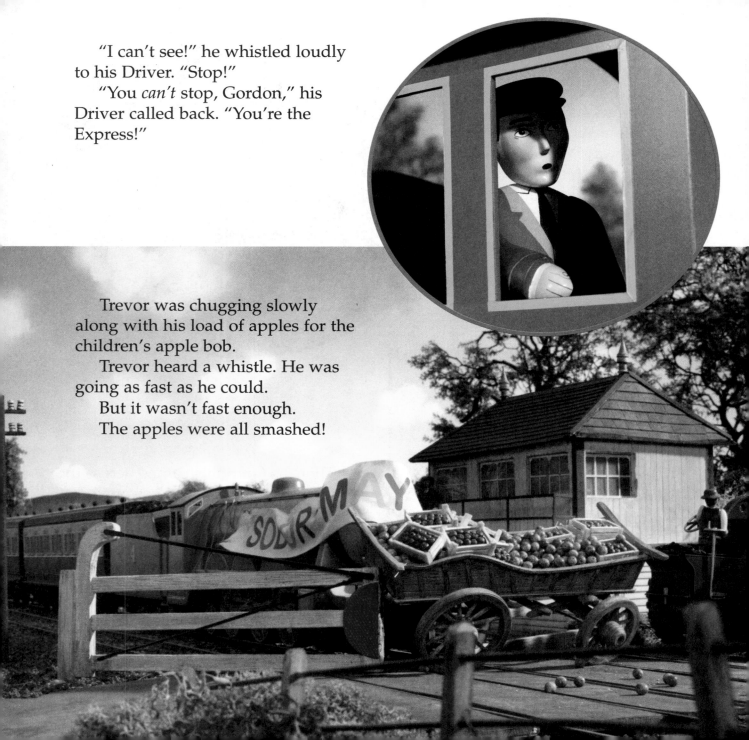

Trevor was chugging slowly along with his load of apples for the children's apple bob.

Trevor heard a whistle. He was going as fast as he could.

But it wasn't fast enough.

The apples were all smashed!

James was the last engine to join the contest—or so he thought!
"Here comes Gordon," cried the passengers.

"We didn't think you wanted to be decorated," teased Thomas.

"I didn't," huffed Gordon.

"Well, you're definitely the Best Dressed Engine," said James.

All the engines agreed.

Gordon was secretly pleased. But he didn't think it was dignified to say so. Silly Gordon!